JACK THE GIANTKILLER

10 9 8 7 6 5 4 3 2 1

British Library Cataloguing in Publication Data available.

ISBN 0 86264 060 1

This book has been printed on acid-free paper

Tony Ross
JACK THE GIANTKILLER

Andersen Press · London

Once, across the Mountains of Imagination and beyond the Valley of Dreams, there lived a terrible giant called Cormoran.

Cormoran was higher than the trees, and he loved to eat sheep, sometimes twenty at one sitting.

In the same shire, there lived a lad called Jack. One day, Jack decided that it was time someone should put a stop to Cormoran and he decided to do it himself.

He went out one night and dug a deep pit at the bottom of Cormoran's mountain.

When it was light, Jack woke the giant by calling insults.

"Hey, SHEEPFACE, CATSBREATH, HOGSFLESH, hey TOMATOHEAD, come down if you DARE!"

With a terrible roar, Cormoran leaped down his mountain, crash, into Jack's pit. There was just enough of him showing above the ground for Jack to hit with his club.

He killed the giant with one blow.

Jack hurried to the town and roused the mayor from his bed.

Jack told the mayor that he had freed the shire of Cormoran.

"How do I know you have?" snapped the mayor, thinking of bed.

"Because I'm wearing his shoes as proof," cried Jack.

The mayor blinked, then he ordered a great rejoicing.

A proclamation was made that from that day Jack should be known as "GIANTKILLER". A sash was made for him with Cormoran's name on it in gold letters.

With his sash, Jack set off to find his fortune.

Now it happened that Cormoran's brother, Blunderbore, lived nearby, and spotted the sun glinting on Jack's sash, as he rested under the trees.

With a roar, Blunderbore sprang on the lad, and locked him in a dungeon, deep below his castle.

But the dungeon was giant-sized, and Jack slipped out through a keyhole. He ran up onto the battlements to look down on Blunderbore, who was showing his castle off to an abominable neighbour.

Quick as a flash, Jack caught the two giants in the ropes that worked the drawbridge. He dangled them in the moat until they drowned, then hung them up to dry.

Pleased with his work, Jack set off to explore the castle.

In a high tower, he found three princesses bound by their own hair.
Blunderbore was keeping them for supper.
Jack cut them free and gave them the keys of the castle.

Jack continued with his journey and that night he came to the castle of a two-headed giant. The giant's name was Elvarach and he seemed a pleasant fellow, for he offered Jack a bed for the night.

After a good supper, Elvarach tucked Jack up in the gigantic guest room and before leaving, looked long and hard at the golden sash.

Jack felt uneasy and lay awake in the huge bed. Before long he heard muttering coming from the giant's room:

"With this club your life I'll take,
Ere from happy dreams you wake."

Putting logs between the sheets, Jack hid under the bed.

At midnight, Elvarach crept into the room and hit the logs again and again.

Next morning, Jack acted as if nothing had happened.

"A couple of gnats landed on my head last night!" he told the amazed Elvarach, vowing revenge on the treacherous giant.

Jack pretended to eat bowl after bowl of porridge for breakfast but really he slipped it into a leather bag concealed under his coat. Then he took a knife and slashed the bag so the porridge spilled onto the floor.

"That's better!" said Jack to the gaping Elvarach. "You ought to try that!"

The silly giant took a knife and plunged it into his own belly.

Jack had killed his fourth giant.

While exploring Elvarach's castle, Jack came to a long flight of
steps. At the bottom a stone hand held an enchanted sword.
The hand offered up the sword without resistance.

Further along the passage, Jack discovered a room full of captives
whom he set free amid much rejoicing.

He gave the castle to the prisoners, as a reward for their years of
misery, and a great party was held.

In the midst of the merrymaking, Elvarach's elder brother, Thunderdell, came visiting. He was furious to see what had happened and demanded to meet the Giantkiller.

At first, Jack quaked at the sight of the ogre. Then he gathered his wits about him. He enraged the giant by pulling funny faces, then turned and fled back inside the castle. He ran to the top of the gatetower and as Thunderdell was crossing the drawbridge, Jack slashed the ropes. The giant crashed down into the moat, where he sank for ever.

Free of the awful brothers, the one-time captives rejoiced and Jack went on his way.

  After travelling for a year and a day, Jack arrived at a misty and desolate mountain, where he met an old man.

  The old man warned Jack to go no further, for ahead lay terrible enchantment and danger.

  "Pooh!" said Jack. "I'm the GIANTKILLER!"

  As the old man could see that Jack would take no warning, he gave him an elfin cloak that would make the wearer invisible.

  When two fiery dragons barred Jack's way, he put on the cloak and slipped by.

The dragons looked quite confused as their dinner vanished.

At the top of the mountain, there was a strange, cold palace, guarded by grotesque statues. Jack shuddered, but called a challenge. A huge door swung open, and out came a magician. All he could see was the enchanted sword, floating in the air. With a terrible scream, he made his escape in a brazen chariot pulled by two dragons.

On the heels of the magician came the biggest giant that Jack had ever seen, but again, the giant couldn't see Jack. The enchanted sword leaped forward, straining in Jack's grasp, and slew the giant.

Jack looked around him and saw a silver horn dangling from a tree. Not knowing what to expect, he blew a fanfare. As he did so, amazing things started happening. The statues took on warm colours and began to stretch and yawn, woken from enchanted sleep. One by one, they turned into their true shapes of lords and knights, with their ladies. They blinked as a golden sun drove away the mists, and they danced with joy as trees and gardens bloomed.

Jack seemed drawn to one statue in particular, not as ugly as the rest. As he watched, the stone trembled and became a graceful hind. Unable to tear his eyes away, Jack watched the hind turn into the loveliest princess he had ever seen.

Of course, they fell in love at once.

The princess told Jack how, years ago, the giant and the magician came to her father's castle and demanded entry. On refusal, the magician turned everybody to stone.

"Only my father escaped," explained the princess, "and he went down the mountain, to wait for someone to come and help us."

"I know, I've met him," said Jack.

Jack knew that his journey was over.
    He married the princess, and they lived together for long, happy lives.